Learning about Feelings with a Unicorn
My Unicorn Books - Volume 7
Written by Steve Herman

Copyright © 2020 by Digital Golden Solutions LLC.
Published by DG Books Publishing, an imprint of
Digital Golden Solutions LLC.

All rights reserved. No part of this publication may be reproduced, distributed, or transmitted in any form or by any means, including photocopying, recording, or other electronic or mechanical methods, without the prior written permission of the publisher, except in the case of brief quotations embodied in critical reviews and certain other noncommercial uses permitted by copyright law.

Information contained within this book is for entertainment and educational purposes only. Although the author and publisher have made every effort to ensure that the information in this book was correct at press time, the author and publisher do not assume and hereby disclaim any liability to any party for any loss, damage, or disruption caused by errors or omissions, whether such errors or omissions result from negligence, accident, or any other cause.

ISBN: 978-1-950280-83-4 (paperback)
ISBN: 978-1-950280-84-1 (hardcover)

www.MyUnicornBooks.com

First Edition: April 2020
10 9 8 7 6 5 4 3 2 1

Hi! I'm Allie McNally, and this is Dazzle D;
Dazzle is a unicorn, as I'm sure that you can see.

It was on a Saturday about a month ago or so
And time for soccer practice, but I didn't want to go.

"What's the matter?" Dazzle asked me. "Why are you so down? Your happy smile has disappeared, and now you wear a frown!"

Dazzle D reminded me that I loved to go to practice. That is when I told her, "Well, Dazzle D, the fact is..."

"Today I don't feel happy, though I know I should be glad – Oh, Dazzle D, what's *wrong* with me? Why must I feel so *bad*?"

Dazzle smiled and nuzzled me (just like I knew she would!) Then told me, "Allie, *feelings* are neither bad nor good."

"Feelings are a part of you, like your fingers and your toes
Or the hair upon your head and the freckles on your nose."

"I'd never seen you so EXCITED! You should have seen your face! You were jumping up and down and danced about the place!"

"One time I remember, Allie, you felt so FRUSTRATED when you wanted to go skiing, and you waited and you waited."

"You thought the time would never come when you could finally go – It's hard to feel much **PATIENCE** when the clock just moves so slow."

"Do you recall the spelling bee when you were feeling SHY? But you competed anyway and gave it your best try;"

"And when you won the spelling bee, remember feeling PROUD When you got the trophy and you heard the cheering crowd?"

"And that made you feel THANKFUL for a friend is like a gift
That's there when you are feeling LOW to give your heart a lift."

"For instance, when you're feeling sad, it's okay to cry,
But know that joy will come again – On that you can rely."

"Don't say hurtful things or throw a hissy fit -
Just breathe deep and count to Ten -
You'll be fine in just a bit!"

"Or when you're feeling worried, remember what I said – Let thoughts of peace and beauty fill your head instead."

"Remember, Allie, any time, you can come to us;
There's no feeling you might have that we cannot discuss."

READ MORE ABOUT ALLIE AND DAZZLE!

VISIT WWW.MYUNICORNBOOKS.COM

OTHER BOOKS BY STEVE HERMAN
MY DRAGON BOOKS SERIES

WWW.MYDRAGONBOOKS.COM

CPSIA information can be obtained
at www.ICGtesting.com
Printed in the USA
BVHW092020240820
587178BV00022B/398